Contents

Chapter	Page

Peter Pan's Arrival

All children grow up except for one strange boy. Wendy knew she would grow up when she was two years old. She had picked a flower and taken it to her mother. Mrs Darling saw her and cried, "Why can't you stay like this forever!"

Wendy realised then, that one day, she would be a grown-up.

Mr and Mrs Darling lived at no. 14. They had three children, Wendy, John and Michael. The Darlings were quite poor, so the nanny they found for their children was a Newfoundland dog called Nana.

Nana was an unusual nanny, but she loved the children dearly. She was there at anytime if one of them needed her. You should have seen her taking the children to school. She walked beside them, butting with her nose if they were naughty.

In the afternoon Nana would join the other nannies waiting at the school for the children. The nannies took no notice of her – they thought her very inferior. Nana in turn thought them rather silly when she heard their gossip.

ISBN 0 86112 822 2
Published by Brimax Books Ltd, Newmarket, England 1992
Printed in Italy.

PETER PAN

ILLUSTRATED BY
ERIC KINCAID

BRIMAX · NEWMARKET · ENGLAND

Introduction

J.M. Barrie's *Peter Pan* was first written in 1904. This wonderful story of make-believe explores a world of fantasy that is familiar to children everywhere.

Peter Pan is the little boy who never wants to grow up. His enchanted life amidst the magical world of the fairies, pirates, mermaids and redskins fascinates Wendy, Michael and John. One night they all fly away to Neverland, where the lost boys live and life is one long, fantastic adventure.

In Neverland, danger and excitement lurk in every shadow. Who knows when the terrible Captain Hook will launch a pirate attack, or where the redskins hide? Only Peter, with his child-like bravery and sense of fun can protect his band of followers.

This beautifully illustrated edition of *Peter Pan* has been specially adapted for younger readers. It perfectly re-creates the magical atmosphere of Neverland and cannot fail to capture the imaginations of those who read it.

The whole family adored Nana, except for Mr Darling, who wondered if people thought them strange having a dog for a nanny. After all he had his position in the city to think about.

All in all the Darlings were a happy family until the arrival of Peter Pan.

Every child has a special world in their mind. It is an island called Neverland, with coral reefs, boats, redskins and hiding places.

Neverland varies a lot in each child's mind. John's Neverland had a lagoon with flamingoes flying over it. Michael's had a flamingo with lagoons flying over it. John lived in an upturned boat, Michael lived in a wigwam. Wendy had a house made of leaves and a pet wolf to keep her company.

Neverland is not a frightening place by day, but just before bedtime, it can seem very real. That's why mothers put night-lights by the bed to stop children becoming frightened.

Mrs Darling always put the children to bed and she would try and find out what they were thinking last thing at night. One name kept appearing in their minds – Peter.

"Who is Peter?" she asked Wendy one night.

"He's Peter Pan," answered Wendy.

Mrs Darling, who had once had her own Neverland, remembered Peter Pan. He lived with the fairies. She was grown up now, but she had believed in him as a child.

"Surely," she said to Wendy, "he's grown up now?"

"Oh, no," said Wendy, who was nearly ten years old. "He's the same size as me." She didn't know how she knew, she just knew.

That evening, Mrs Darling mentioned Peter Pan to her husband.

"It's only some nonsense that Nana has put in their heads," said Mr Darling.

But life was not as easy as that and Mrs Darling had quite a shock a few days later.

Wendy gave her some leaves that she had found in the nursery. The leaves came from a strange tree and had not been in the nursery the night before.

9

"I think it is Peter Pan again," said Wendy.

"What do you mean, Wendy?" asked her mother.

"The leaves must have been on his shoes," said Wendy. "He really should have wiped his feet before he came in."

Wendy told her mother how she thought Peter came into the nursery at night and sat on the end of the bed.

"But nobody can get into the house without knocking," said Mrs Darling.

"He doesn't knock," said Wendy. "I think he comes in through the window."

"But we're three floors up, in the nursery," said her mother.

"The leaves were by the window, weren't they?" said Wendy.

Mrs Darling looked at the leaves. Had there been someone in the nursery?

"Wendy must be dreaming," she said.

But Wendy was not dreaming and the next evening, Mrs Darling had another shock.

Mrs Darling had put the children to bed with a song and a story, then she had sat by the fire and dozed off. She dreamed she could see Wendy, Michael and John peering through the clouds at Neverland. The dream was strange, but what happened next was stranger still.

The window blew open and a boy dropped onto the floor. There was a tiny light with him, that flitted here and there. It was this that woke Mrs Darling. She woke with a cry and saw the boy.

She knew at once that he was Peter Pan. He was dressed in an outfit made of leaves. At that moment, Nana came into the nursery. She leapt at the boy who jumped through the window.

Mrs Darling was worried what may have happened to the boy. They were three floors up! She ran downstairs, but there was no sign of him. She returned to the nursery to find Nana with something in her mouth.

It was the boy's shadow. Nana had closed the window on the boy, but had only caught his shadow. Nana put the shadow outside the window,

10

for the boy to collect. But Mrs Darling rolled it up and put it in a drawer. She wanted to tell Mr Darling about the boy, but her chance did not come until the following Friday.

They had been invited out to dinner, and were getting ready to go, while the children were getting ready for bed.

Mrs Darling had gone to the nursery to show Wendy her dress. Wendy had lent her mother her bracelet and was very proud when she saw her wearing it. Then Mr Darling walked in looking furious. In his hand he held a tie.

"What's the matter?" asked Mrs Darling.

"The matter is this tie. Unless it is round my neck soon, we won't go out for dinner," he said.

"Let me try," said Mrs Darling, and the tie was done in no time. Everyone was happy until Nana wandered in and brushed against Mr Darling's new trousers. Mr Darling was furious and said how silly it was to have a dog as a nanny.

As Mrs Darling was brushing off the hairs, she had a sudden thought and told Mr Darling about the boy who had been in the nursery. She showed him the shadow.

"He does look a bit of a scoundrel," said Mr Darling.

At that moment, Nana returned with some medicine for Michael. She poured it into a spoon but Michael would not take it.

"When I was your age," said Mr Darling, "I always took my medicine."

"Father still has to take medicine," said Wendy.

"It's horrible," said Mr Darling. "I'd take it now if I hadn't lost the bottle."

Mr Darling hadn't lost the medicine, he had hidden it, but Liza, the maid had found it and put it back on the bedside table. Wendy had seen it there.

"I know where it is," she cried. Wendy returned with some in a glass.

"Michael, you take yours first," said Mr Darling.

"No, Father, you first," said Michael.

"I shall be sick," said Mr Darling. "There's more in my glass than in your spoon."

11

"You said you could take yours easily," said Wendy.

"I'm waiting, Father," said Michael.

"Why don't you both take it together," suggested Wendy.

"Certainly," said Mr Darling, "Ready, Michael?"

"One, two, three," counted Wendy. Michael took his medicine, but Mr Darling slipped his behind his back. Michael howled with rage.

"Stop that, Michael," said Mr Darling. "I've already had some medicine today. I'll pour it into Nana's bowl instead, she'll think it's some milk."

The children did not smile as he poured his medicine into the bowl. Nana returned a few moments later.

"Nana," said Mr Darling. "There is some milk in your bowl."

Nana lapped the medicine from her bowl then gave Mr Darling a very hurt look. Wendy ran and put her arms round her.

"It was only a joke," mumbled Mr Darling. "That dog will not lord it in my nursery. Her proper place is in the yard. She must go there now."

The children cried. Mrs Darling said, "Remember what happened the other night – that strange boy."

"My mind is made up," said Mr Darling and he dragged Nana downstairs to the yard.

Mrs Darling put the children to bed and lit their night-lights. They could hear Nana barking.

"That's not Nana's unhappy bark, that's her 'I smell danger' bark," said Wendy.

"Are you sure?" said Mrs Darling. She checked the window. It was securely locked, but she still felt uncomfortable.

"I wish I wasn't going out tonight," she said.

"Nothing can hurt us if the night-lights are burning," yawned Michael.

"Nothing at all," said Mrs Darling.

She sang lullabies until the children were asleep and then she crept from the room.

Mr and Mrs Darling left the house. The stars looked on. As soon as the grown-ups were out of sight, the smallest star screamed, "Now, Peter!"

The Flight to Neverland

After Mr and Mrs Darling left, the night-lights continued to burn, then they winked out one by one. But there was another light in the room that burned much brighter. It flashed about from drawer to cupboard looking for Peter's shadow. But it was not really a light. It was a fairy called Tinker Bell.

A moment later, the window opened and Peter Pan dropped in. He had carried Tinker Bell part of the way and still had fairy dust on his hands.

"Tinker Bell," he called. "Where are you? Have you found my shadow yet?"

Peter looked all around the room for Tinker Bell. Suddenly he heard a tinkle of golden bells, Peter understood fairy language and knew that Tinker Bell was telling him she had found the shadow in a drawer in the big box. He realised she meant the chest of drawers and finding his shadow, he shut the drawer again. He didn't know that Tinker Bell was still inside.

Peter thought that his shadow would stick back in place, but it didn't. It just lay on the floor. He took some soap from the bathroom and tried to stick it on with that, but it didn't work. He thought he would never be able to join his shadow again. He sat on the floor and cried. His sobs woke Wendy and she sat up in bed. She wasn't surprised to see a stranger on the floor.

"Boy," she said, "why are you crying?"

Peter stood and bowed. Wendy was delighted and bowed in turn.

"What's your name?" the boy asked.

"Wendy Darling," replied Wendy. "What's yours?"

"Peter Pan," said Peter.

Wendy had already guessed this.

"Why are you crying?" she asked again.

"I can't stick my shadow on," said Peter. "Anyway, I wasn't crying."

According to Peter, he never cried and he never slept.

13

Wendy saw the shadow on the floor and felt sorry for Peter.

"I'll sew your shadow on for you," she said. She fetched a needle and thread and sewed the shadow back on to Peter's foot. Peter was delighted and he crowed with pleasure. He had already forgotten who had helped him.

"What a clever boy I am!" he cried.

"I suppose I had nothing to do with it?" asked Wendy.

"You helped a little," said Peter.

Wendy got back in to bed and said, "in that case, if you have no more use for me, I shall go back to sleep."

Peter tried to get her to look up by pretending to leave. When that failed he said, "I'm sorry, I just crow like that when I am pleased with myself."

Wendy still wouldn't look up. Peter put on his angelic voice.

"Wendy," he said. "One girl is more use than twenty boys."

"Do you think so?" asked Wendy. Peter's charm had worked. Wendy sat down beside him again.

"I will give you a kiss, if you like," Wendy said to Peter.

Peter held out his hand for a kiss. Wendy was sad when she realised Peter did not know what a kiss was.

"Surely you know what a kiss is?" she said.

"I'll know when you give it to me," said Peter.

Wendy did not want to hurt Peter's feelings, so she gave him a thimble instead.

"Shall I give you a kiss?" asked Peter.

"If you please," said Wendy.

Peter took an acorn button and put it in her hand.

"I'll wear it on a chain around my neck," said Wendy.

Wendy asked Peter how old he was.

"Quite young, I think," he said. "I ran away the day I was born. I heard my mother and father talking about what I would be when I was a man. I did not want to be a man so I decided to run away

14

*Wendy saw the shadow on the floor
and felt sorry for Peter.*

to Kensington Gardens and lived with the fairies."

Wendy asked question after question about the fairies. Peter was surprised because he had always thought that fairies were boring. He liked them on the whole and told Wendy how the fairies began.

"When the first baby laughed, its laugh broke into a thousand tiny pieces and each piece became a fairy. There's supposed to be a fairy for every girl and boy."

"Supposed to be?" asked Wendy. "Isn't there?"

"No. Children know so much nowadays, they don't believe in fairies. Every time one says, 'I don't believe in fairies', a fairy somewhere drops down dead."

Peter began to wonder where Tinker Bell was.

"I can't think where she has got to," he said.

Wendy looked around her, "Are you telling me that there is a fairy in here?"

"She was here a moment ago," said Peter. "Can't you hear her?"

"I can hear bells," said Wendy.

"That's her," said Peter. "I can hear her now, that's fairy language." The sound came from the chest of drawers.

"I think I shut her in the drawer," said Peter. He let Tinker Bell out of the drawer and she flew around the room screaming with fury.

"I'm sorry, Tink," said Peter. "How was I supposed to know that you were in there."

"If only she would stand still long enough for me to look at her," said Wendy.

Fairies rarely stand still, but Tinker Bell paused for a moment on the nursery clock. Wendy was delighted, but Tinker Bell did not like Wendy. Peter had been talking to her for far too long.

"She's quite a common fairy really," said Peter. "She's called Tinker Bell because she mends the pots and kettles like gypsy tinkers do."

Wendy was full of questions. "If you don't live in Kensington Gardens now . . ."

"I do sometimes," Peter interrupted.

"Where do you live mostly, then?" asked Wendy.

"I live with the lost boys," said Peter. "They are

16

children who fall out of their prams when they are small. If no one claims them in seven days they are sent to Neverland. I'm their captain."

Wendy thought it must be great fun in Neverland. Peter began to tell Wendy why he had come to the nursery window. It was to listen to the stories that Mrs Darling told the children.

"I don't know any stories," said Peter. "What happened the other night, to the Prince who could not find the lady who wore the glass slipper?"

"That was Cinderella!" said Wendy. "The Prince found her and they lived happily ever after."

Peter seemed delighted and rushed to the window.

"Where are you going?" asked Wendy.

"To tell the lost boys what happened."

"Don't go, Peter," said Wendy.

"Come with me," said Peter. "Come with me to Neverland and tell the boys more stories."

He began to pull her towards the window.

"I can't fly," said Wendy.

"I'll teach you," said Peter.

"Oo! How lovely to fly," said Wendy.

"There are mermaids," said Peter.

"Mermaids!" said Wendy.

Peter was being very clever, he wanted Wendy to fly away with him.

"You can tuck us in at night and make pockets for us. None of us has any pockets."

"Can you teach John and Michael to fly as well?" cried Wendy.

"If you like," said Peter.

Wendy rushed to wake her brothers.

"Wake up!" she cried. "Peter's going to teach us how to fly."

Peter signalled for quiet. There was silence, not a sound could be heard. Nana had been barking all evening, but now she was quiet.

"Quick, hide!" called John.

Nana burst into the nursery, dragging Liza, the maid, behind her. Liza glanced round.

"They are all fast asleep," she said.

Nana knew the children were behind the curtains, but she was hauled away and tied up again.

17

In the nursery, the children watched as Peter flew around the room.

"How do you do it?" asked John.

"Just think wonderful thoughts," said Peter. Of course it was not as simple as that. It also took fairy dust and Peter still had some on his hands from carrying Tinker Bell. He blew some onto the children. The children were holding onto their beds.

"Just wriggle your shoulders and let go," said Peter.

Michael drifted to the ceiling.

"I can fly!" he squealed.

"So can I," cried John.

"Me too," said Wendy.

The children flew clumsily around the room and every time Peter tried to help Wendy, Tinker Bell grew more angry.

"Why don't we go out?" said John.

This was just what Peter wanted, but Wendy hesitated.

"Mermaids!" called Peter. Wendy needed to hear no more.

"Pirates!" said Peter, and Michael grabbed his best Sunday hat.

Nana broke free from her ropes as Mr and Mrs Darling were returning. They looked up to the nursery window. The room was ablaze with light and there were three figures flying round and round. But wait! There were four figures not three!

The stars were watching and a small one called, "Watch out, Peter!" and blew the window open again.

Peter soared into the sky, followed by John, Michael and Wendy.

Mr and Mrs Darling rushed into the nursery but the children had gone.

"Second on the right and straight on till morning." Peter had told Wendy that this was the way to Neverland, but Peter often just said the first thing that came into his head.

At first the children trusted Peter as they flew around spires and domes. Wendy wondered how far they had flown. John began to wonder the same thing

18

when they were flying over their second sea, or was it their third night? None of the children knew how much time had passed. When they were hungry Peter chased the birds with food in their mouths and snatched it from them. Then the birds would try and snatch it back.

When the children slept, the moment they closed their eyes, down they fell. Peter thought this was very funny.

"There he goes," he laughed as Michael fell towards the sea.

"Save him!" cried Wendy. Peter would dive through the air and catch Michael just before he hit the water. He always waited till the last moment.

After days of flying they reached Neverland.

"There it is," said Peter.

Arrows of light from the sun were pointing out the island for the children. All three looked ahead to get their first glimpse.

"John," cried Wendy. "There's the lagoon."

"Yes," said Michael. "And there's your flamingo."

John spotted Michael's cave and they all saw Wendy's pet wolf. Michael saw the redskin camp.

Night was falling and the children were a little nervous.

"Do you want tea or an adventure?" asked Peter.

Wendy and Michael wanted tea, but John asked, "What sort of adventure?"

"There's a pirate below," said Peter. "We could kill him."

"Do you kill many?" cried John.

"Tons," said Peter. "I have never known so many on this island before."

"Who is their captain?" asked John.

"Captain Hook."

"How big is he?" asked John.

"Not as big as he used to be," said Peter. "I cut a bit off him."

"What bit?" asked John.

"His right hand," said Peter.

"Then he can't fight," said John.

"He can," said Peter. "He has a hook now instead. You must promise me one thing. If it comes to a

19

fight. Leave him to me."

"I promise," said John.

Then Peter said, "Tink can't fly as slowly as us and with all her flying backwards and forwards the pirates have seen her and spotted us. They've pulled out Long Tom, the cannon. They're sure to fire at us as they've seen Tink."

"Tell her to go away," cried the children.

"She's scared, too," said Peter. "I can't send her away."

"Tell her to put out her light," said Wendy.

"She can't," said Peter. "Only when she's asleep,"

Peter solved the problem. Tinker Bell sat in Michael's hat and Wendy held it. Tinker Bell hated being carried by Wendy.

They flew on in the darkness. It was very quiet.

"BOOM!" The silence was shattered by Long Tom. Everyone was sent flying through the heavens. No one was hit, but Peter was blown out to sea. John and Michael found themselves alone in the darkness. Wendy still had Tinker Bell, but it may have been better if she hadn't.

20

The Island of Neverland

Whenever Peter returns to Neverland, the island comes to life.

Everyone was on the move. The lost boys were looking for Peter, the pirates were out looking for the lost boys, the redskins were out looking for the pirates and the beasts were looking for the redskins. They were going round and round the island at the same speed, in the same direction, so they did not meet.

All wanted blood except the lost boys. They just wanted their captain, Peter Pan.

The number of boys varies. It depends on who has been killed and who is growing up. Growing up is against Peter's rules and he thins the boys out from time to time. Tonight there are six boys, each with a dagger in his hand. They all wear bearskins, which Peter likes, as he wants no one to dress like him.

The first is Tootles, the gentlest of the boys. He always misses what happens to the others, by going round a corner on his own and returning to find the other boys have had an adventure. But Tink thinks he is the easiest to trick, so he had better watch out tonight.

Next comes Nibs, a cheerful lad. Then there is Slightly, who can cut whistles out of wood. Curly

is next. He's forever in trouble and he often takes the blame when one of the others is naughty.

Finally there are the twins. Peter could not understand twins and because of this, no one else in the band knew much about them either.

As the boys walk off in the dark of the forest, a song can be heard some distance behind them:

"Avast below, yo ho, heave to,
A-pirating we will go,
And if we're parted by a shot,
We're sure to meet below!"

It was the pirates. There was never a more villainous-looking lot, armed to the teeth with pistols, cutlasses and daggers. There was the Italian Cecco, with coins in his ears as ornaments. Behind Cecco, the giant Blackamoor, then Bill Jukes, who's covered in tattoos. Here comes gentleman Starkey, once a highborn schoolboy.

Behind him is Skylight, and the Bo'sun Smee, who always apologises to any man he is about to kill.

In the middle of this gang of pirates, sitting on a chair being carried by his men, is the blackest cut-throat of them all – Captain James Hook. He's a huge man with long, dark, curly hair and a hook instead of his right hand.

On the trail of the pirates come the redskins. They carry tomahawks and knives. They're from the Piccaninny tribe and hanging from their belts are the scalps of boys as well as pirates. Great Big Little Panther is leading and at the end of the column comes Tiger Lily, the beautiful redskin princess.

Out of the shadows, behind the redskins come the beasts. There are lions, tigers, bears and other savage animals.

Finally, when they have passed, there is one more beast to come, a gigantic crocodile.

The boys were first to break the circle. They suddenly sat down on the grass.

"I wish Peter would come home soon," said Nibs.

There was never a more villainous-looking lot,
armed to the teeth with pistols, cutlasses and daggers.

The boys were suddenly silent as they heard the pirate song in the distance. Then they disappeared into their underground home. Each boy had his own hollow tree trunk to climb into to get below ground. Hook had been looking for this secret hideout for many years.

Nibs decided to keep an eye on the pirates, but one of them spotted him and drew his pistol.

"Put that away!" cried Hook. "Do you want the redskins on us? That was only one boy, I want them all. Especially Peter Pan. He's the one who cut off my hand."

Hook looked proudly at the hook. "Do you know what he did with my arm?" he asked Smee. "He fed it to a crocodile."

"I have noticed how you fear crocodiles," said Smee.

"Only one," said Hook. "He's got the taste for me and follows me around. Luckily he swallowed a ticking clock, which still ticks inside him, so I can hear him coming."

"The tick will run out one day," said Smee.

"Aye, I know," said Hook.

Hook was sitting on a large toadstool. He suddenly leapt up. "I'm burning!" he cried. He kicked at the toadstool which fell over revealing a hole with smoke coming out of it and the sound of children's voices.

"A chimney!" cried Hook. They had found the lost boys' underground home. As they looked around they found seven hollow trees.

"We must bake a cake, poison it and leave it for the lost boys to find," said Hook.

A sudden 'Tick! Tick! Tick!' stopped them in their tracks. Hook stood shaking with fear.

"The crocodile," he whispered and fled.

The boys came out of hiding. Nibs looked up.

"I can see a great white bird," he said. "It keeps saying 'Poor Wendy'."

"It's a Wendy bird," said Slightly. "I remember them."

The boys could hear Wendy, but they could also hear Tinker Bell.

"Peter wants you to kill the Wendy bird," she called.

The boys always did what Peter wanted and they ran underground to fetch their weapons. All except Tootles, who was still carrying his bow and arrow.

"Quick, Tootles," cried Tinker Bell. "Peter will be so pleased."

Tootles dropped to one knee and fired an arrow. It hit Wendy and she fell to the ground.

Tootles stood over Wendy's body and waited for the others to return.

"You're too late," he said proudly. "I've already killed the Wendy bird."

Tinker Bell flew off.

The boys crowded around Wendy.

Slightly spoke first. "This isn't a bird. It's a lady."

"And Tootles killed her," said Nibs.

Tootles face was white as he moved away. He was scared of Peter.

At that moment they heard Peter crowing. The boys gathered round Wendy to hide her, but Tootles stood to one side.

"Greetings, boys," he said. "I've brought a mother for you. Have you seen her?"

"Stand back boys and let Peter see," said Tootles quietly.

Peter looked at Wendy, he knelt down and removed the arrow. "Whose is this?" he asked.

25

"It's mine," said Tootles.

Peter was going to hit Tootles with the arrow, but something stopped him.

The boys looked and saw that Wendy had hold of Peter's arm.

"Poor Tootles," they heard her whisper.

"She's alive," said Peter. He suddenly saw the acorn button that he had given Wendy. "Look!" he cried. "It's the kiss I gave her. It saved her life!"

Peter begged Wendy to get better. "Remember the mermaids," he said.

There was a cry in the sky. It was Tinker Bell.

The boys told Peter of Tinker Bell's crime.

"You're no longer my fairy," he called out. "Be gone forever."

Tinker Bell flew down to Peter's shoulder, begging for forgiveness. Wendy moved a bit more.

"Well maybe for just a week," he said.

The boys were talking about moving Wendy to their underground home.

"We can't move her," said Peter. "We must build a house around her."

As the boys got to work, Michael and John arrived. Peter had completely forgotten about them.

"Is Wendy asleep?" asked John.

"Yes," said Peter. "Curly, these two boys will help build the house."

"Build the house?" said John.

"A house for Wendy," said Curly.

"For Wendy!" cried John. "She's only a girl!"

"That's why we're her servants," said Curly.

"Yes," said Peter. "And you will be, too. We must build a house around Wendy."

The amazed brothers were set to work on cutting wood to build the house. Peter wanted a doctor to look at Wendy. He sent Slightly to find one.

Slightly had no idea where to find one, but he saw John's top hat and had a sudden idea. He put it on and turned back to Peter.

"Are you the doctor?" asked Peter. He often played pretend with the boys, but sometimes real

26

life and pretend became a bit muddled.

"Yes I am," said Slightly. "I will put this glass thing in the patient's mouth. That should cure her."

Slightly bent over Wendy and put a pretend glass thing in her mouth.

"How is she?" asked Peter.

"She will get better," said Slightly. "I'll come back this evening to see her again. Goodbye." And Slightly left, relieved that Peter had believed him.

Everything was ready for the house building. Wendy told them what she wanted and the boys set to work. She wanted funny red walls and a roof of mossy green, with roses at the door.

For the final touches, Tootles gave up the sole of his shoe for the knocker and John's top hat became the chimney.

The boys then tidied themselves and knocked on the door. Wendy opened it and invited them all in. Even though the house was small, everyone fitted in.

Later on, Wendy tucked them up in their great bed in the underground home, but she slept in her house. Peter sat outside on guard. He had heard the pirates singing far away and was sure there were wolves nearby.

Needless to say, he soon fell asleep and while he slept fairies took great delight in tweaking his nose as they passed by on their way home to their nests in the treetops.

The Mermaids' Lagoon

Next morning, Peter measured Michael, John and Wendy for their own hollow trees to the underground home.

Peter made sure the person fitted the tree by making alterations to them. Wendy and Michael fitted their trees first time, but John had to be altered slightly.

After a few days, the children could go up and down their trees as quickly as the boys. They loved their new home. It was just one room, with mushrooms on the floor that were used as stools. A Never tree grew in the middle of the room. Every morning it was sawn to the floor. By tea time it was high enough to be used as a table.

There was one large bed that all the boys slept in, except Michael. Wendy wanted a baby and as Michael was the smallest he had to be the baby and sleep in a basket hanging from the ceiling.

Tinker Bell also lived in the underground home in a small opening in the wall. Tink's room was beautiful, with carpets, rugs and a twinkling chandelier.

Wendy met her pet wolf soon after her arrival. The wolf soon followed Wendy wherever she went. Wendy occassionally thought of home. What worried her was that John was beginning to forget what his parents looked like. Michael was happy to believe that Wendy was his mother.

The children had many adventures. One day, in the middle of a fight against the redskins, Peter decided to change sides.

"I'm a redskin," he told Tootles. "What are you?" Tootles became a redskin too. Soon all the children were redskins. The redskins joined in with Peter's game and became lost boys for a while.

Another time, several of the redskins became trapped in the hollow trees in an attack on the underground home and had to be popped out.

28

There is a bird on Neverland called the Never bird. One of these birds built its nest in a tree over-hanging the lagoon. One day, the nest, eggs and bird fell in the water. But the nest floated and the Never bird would not abandon her eggs.

Peter was impressed and ordered that the Never bird should be left alone. The Never bird would reward Peter for this kindness one day.

One of the most exciting adventures involved the redskin princess, Tiger Lily. It happened at the Mermaids' Lagoon, where the children often spent long summer days. Wendy was fascinated by the mermaids, but they wouldn't play with the children. The only one to get close to them was Peter. He chatted with them at Marooners' Rock and would even sit on their tails if they were cheeky.

The most haunting time to see the mermaids was in the evening when they would sing their strange songs. The lagoon was a dangerous place then. Wendy had never been there at that time of day because she always made sure the boys were in bed by seven.

One day, they were all lazing about at the lagoon when Wendy suddenly heard the sound of oars. She froze to the spot. She could not even move to wake the children.

As she listened to the oars she remembered how Marooners' Rock had earned its name. Evil captains had left sailors to drown on it because when the tide rises, the rock is covered by water.

Fortunately, Peter could smell danger even in his sleep. He leapt up and stood listening.

"Pirates!" he cried.

The other boys jumped up, ready to obey their captain.

"Dive!" said Peter, and all the children dived into the water.

The boat came closer. Inside were Smee, Starkey and the redskin princess, Tiger Lily. Her hands and feet were bound. She was to be left on the rock to drown.

The pirates crashed the boat into Marooners' Rock and the redskin princess was thrown onto it.

*The most haunting time to see the mermaids
is in the evening when they would sing their strange songs.*

Two heads bobbed in the water near the rock. Wendy was crying, thinking that Tiger Lily was about to drown. Peter was angry. It was two pirates against one redskin, which wasn't fair.

He didn't wait for the boat to leave. He called out to Smee and Starkey, imitating Hook's voice.

"Ahoy there!" he called.

"It's the captain," said Smee. "We've put Tiger Lily on the rock," he called out.

"Well, you can cut her free now," said Peter.

"Free?" asked the pirates.

"Yes," said Peter. "Or you'll feel my hook!"

"Aye, aye," said Smee, and he cut Tiger Lily's ropes. She slipped into the water and swam away.

Peter thought he had been extremely clever and was about to crow his success. Wendy covered his mouth with her hand. At that moment, Hook's voice rang out over the gloomy lagoon. He swam up to the boat and his men helped him on board. Smee and Starkey were curious to know why their captain was there. They waited in silence.

"The game's up!" Hook cried. "The boys have a mother."

"A mother?" cried Starkey.

"What is a mother?" asked Smee. Wendy's heart went out to Smee for not knowing what a mother was.

"That is a mother," said Hook, as the Never bird floated by on her nest. "She stays with her eggs come what may."

"Captain," said Smee, "why don't we kidnap the boys' mother, so that she will be our mother?"

"A brilliant idea!" said Hook. "We will catch them all. The boys can walk the plank and we will have a mother!"

On hearing this, Wendy cried out, "Never!"

The pirates looked around but could see nothing, and decided it was the wind. Hook suddenly remembered Tiger Lily.

"Where's the redskin?" he asked.

"Free, as you said, Captain," said Smee.

"Free!" cried Hook. "What do you mean?"

"You gave the order," said Starkey.

The pirates looked around but could see nothing.

"I gave no such order," said Hook. "What is happening here?"

The pirates looked around uneasily.

"There must be a spirit haunting the lagoon," said Hook. "Spirit, do you hear me?" he called.

Peter immediately answered in Hook's voice, "Odds, bobs, hammer and tongs, I hear you."

The pirates were terrified.

"Who are you?" cried Hook.

"Captain James Hook," said Peter, enjoying himself.

"You're not!" cried Hook. "If you are, who am I?"

"A codfish!" came the answer.

"A codfish!" exclaimed Hook. "Do you have another voice and name?"

"I have," answered Peter in his own voice.

"Vegetable?" asked Hook.

"No."

"Animal?"

"Yes."

"Man?"

"No!" exclaimed Peter.

"Boy?"

"Yes."

"Ordinary boy?"

"No!"

"Wonderful boy?"

"Yes!" cried Peter. "Do you give up?"

The pirates gave up.

"I'm Peter Pan," cried Peter.

"Pan!" cried Hook. "Get him!"

Hook leapt out of the boat to attack Peter. Peter called out, "Are you ready boys?" The lost boys came swimming from all corners of the lagoon.

They attacked the pirates with swords drawn. The battle was short. There were only the two pirates in the boat and they made a hasty retreat from the boys' sharp swords. After that they turned to Hook and surrounded him. They kept a good distance from the dangerous hook.

Only one was brave enough to fight him and that was Peter. They were both pulling themselves onto the rock when they came face to face.

34

Peter was not scared. He grabbed a knife from Hook's belt and was about to use it when he saw he was higher up the rock than his enemy. This was not fair and he put out his hand to help the pirate up.

Hook paid Peter back by biting him. Peter was amazed, because he had tried to help Hook. Hook then clawed Peter with his hook and it seemed as though Peter was going to die.

'Tick! Tick! Tick! Tick!' Hook heard the familiar sound. His face turned white. He dived into the water and swam for the ship, with the crocodile on his tail!

The boys were searching for Peter Pan and Wendy. As they couldn't find them, they thought they must have gone home before them.

Wendy had fainted and Peter had to drag her onto the rock.

"Wendy," said Peter, "we're on the rock. It will be covered soon. We must go."

"Shall we swim or fly?" asked Wendy.

"I'm wounded," said Peter. "Can you fly or swim on your own?"

Wendy shook her head.

At that moment, a piece of string dropped in front of them. It was the tail of Michael's kite, which had pulled away from him in a strong wind.

Peter tied the tail around Wendy. The wind carried the kite and lifted Wendy from the rock.

Peter was left alone to listen to the mermaids and to wonder what it would be like to die.

"It will be a great adventure," he said aloud.

35

Peter watched the mermaids disappear one by one. The water was rising around the rock. It was beginning to lap at his feet.

To pass the time, Peter watched the only moving object on the lagoon. From a distance, it looked like a scrap of paper floating in the water. But there was something strange about it. It seemed to be fighting the tide and Peter was always happy to cheer the underdog. He clapped everytime the piece of paper gained ground.

Of course, it wasn't paper. It was the Never bird. She was desperately trying to reach Peter. She was determined to save him even if it meant losing her eggs. She was exhausted by the time she reached the rock.

She called out to Peter, trying to tell him what she was doing. Peter did not understand a word she said. "What are you doing?" he asked.

"I want you to get into the nest," said the bird as slowly and as clearly as possible. "Can you swim to me?"

"What are you quacking about?" asked Peter.

"You stupid boy!" she yelled. "I'm trying to help."

Peter was sure she was calling him names and he shouted back. Then they both shouted at each other, "Shut up!"

The bird was determined to help Peter, however and she paddled closer to the rock and then flew up into the air.

Peter suddenly realised what she was doing and jumped into the nest. Inside were two eggs. The Never bird couldn't bear to watch. But Peter was busy thinking. Starkey had hung his hat from a pole on the rock. Peter put the eggs inside the hat and set it on the water. The Never bird was delighted and settled on her new nest.

Peter floated off in one direction and the Never bird went in another. The nest took Peter to land and he left it there for the Never bird to reclaim, but she was delighted with her new nest. The strange thing is that Never birds now always build their nests in the shape of a hat.

Peter floated off in one direction and the Never bird went in the other.

The Happy Home

Following the adventure at Marooners' Rock, the redskins became the boys' greatest friends. Peter had saved Tiger Lily's life and there was nothing they would not do for him.

Everynight they stood guard outside the underground home, watching out for the pirate attack which everyone knew would soon come.

Wendy sympathised with the boys, but she was a loyal house-wife. "Father knows best," she would say, but even she did not really like being called a squaw.

One evening, when the redskins were in their guarding positions, the children were in their underground home having their evening meal. Peter was out getting the time for Wendy. The way to do this was to follow the crocodile and wait for the clock to strike the hour.

The evening meal was make-believe, so the children were enjoying eating everything they could possibly think of. They were not allowed to argue at the table, but they could still complain.

"Have you finished your milk, Slightly?" asked Wendy.

"Nearly," said Slightly, looking into his imaginary cup.

"He hasn't," said Nibs.

Slightly's hand shot up. "I complain of Nibs."

But at the same time, John asked a question. "Can I sit in Father's chair?"

"Certainly not," said Wendy. "Only Father sits there."

"He's not really our father," muttered John. "I had to tell him what a father is."

"We complain of John," cried the twins. They thought he was complaining too much.

"I don't suppose I could be father?" asked Tootles quietly.

Wendy was always gentle with Tootles. "No, dear, I'm afraid you can't."

"Can I be baby, then?" Tootles asked Michael.

"No," said Michael from his hanging basket.

"Can I be a twin?"

"Oh, no. It's very difficult being a twin," said the twins.

"Does anyone want to see me do a trick, then?" he asked.

"No!" was the answer.

Wendy finally told the boys to clear the table and settled down to do some sewing and darning.

The boys began to dance around the room and Peter returned to this happy scene. He had nuts for the boys and the time for Wendy.

"Dance with us," one of the twins said to Peter.

"What!" said Peter, who was really the best dancer. "My old bones would rattle."

"Please," said Slightly, "It is Saturday night."

Whether it was Saturday night or not, the children did not know as they had lost all track of the days. But to them, a special night was Saturday night and soon they were all dancing and singing.

Later on, as the boys were getting ready for bed, Peter asked Wendy a question. "It is only make-believe that I am their father, isn't it?"

"Oh, yes," said Wendy.

"It would make me seem very old if I was their father," said Peter.

"But the boys are ours," said Wendy.

"But not really," said Peter, a little worried.

"Not if you don't want them to be," said Wendy. "But Peter, what do you think of me?"

"I'm your devoted son," said Peter.

Wendy had known the answer. Peter would never grow up. She would have to be his mother.

"It's funny," said Peter. "Tiger Lily is the same. She doesn't want to be my mother. Maybe Tinker Bell will be."

"Silly boy," said Tink and Wendy was inclined to agree with her.

When the boys were finally ready for bed, they settled down to listen to Wendy's story. It was the one the boys loved, but Peter hated it.

Usually he left the room, but this time he stayed. If he had gone, things may have turned out differently.

"I'll begin," said Wendy, with the boys settled all around her. "There once was a man . . ."

"I wish it were a lady," said Curly.

"Or a white rat," said Nibs.

"Ssh," said Wendy. "There was a lady, too. The man's name was Mr Darling and the lady was Mrs Darling."

"I think I know them," said Michael.

"What do you think they had?" asked Wendy.

"White rats?" suggested Nibs.

"No," said Wendy. "They had three children and a faithful nurse called Nana. One night all the children flew away to Neverland where the lost children are."

"Wendy!" asked Tootles. "Was one of the lost boys called Tootles?"

"Yes, he was," said Wendy.

"I'm in a story!" cried Tootles.

"Ssh," said Wendy. "Now think how sad Mr and Mrs Darling were. Think of the empty beds."

"This is a very sad story," said the twins.

"Will there be a happy ending?" asked Nibs.

"If you know about a mother's love," said Wendy.

"You'll know there'll be a happy ending."

Peter hated to hear about mothers and he hated this part of the story. Wendy continued. "The heroine of this story knows that the nursery window will always be open for the children to return. That's why the children stayed away for so long."

"Did they go back?" asked Nibs.

The children were delighted when Wendy told them that the heroine of the story was herself and she went on with her story. "Wendy and her brothers flew back and the window was open and there was never a happier scene," she finished.

Peter groaned. He hated this talk about mothers.

"You're wrong about mothers, Wendy," he said.

The boys gathered around Peter to hear what he had to say.

"I used to think like Wendy. I always thought my mother would keep the window open for me. I stayed away a long time. When I tried to go back, the window was shut. My mother had forgotten all about me and another little boy was asleep in my bed."

Whether this was true or not, Peter couldn't say but he believed what he was saying at that moment.

"Are mothers really like that?" asked the boys.

"Oh, yes," said Peter.

"Let's go home now," said Michael.

"Yes," said Wendy, holding her brothers close to her. "Mother might think we're never coming back."

Wendy forgot about Peter's feelings at that moment and asked rather sharply if he would make the arrangements.

"If you wish," Peter replied, coolly. He was angry with grown-ups for spoiling things again. He hurried to his tree and went up.

The boys began to panic, they didn't want to lose their mother. "We can't let her go," said one.

"Make her our prisoner," said another.

Wendy looked to Tootles for help. He didn't fail her. "I may be just Tootles," he said. "But if anyone touches Wendy, he'll get a bloody nose from me."

Peter returned just then. "I've spoken to the

41

redskins. They'll guide you through the wood."

Peter then told Nibs to wake Tinker Bell. Tink had been listening and was glad that Wendy was going, but she was sure she wasn't going to be the one to lead Wendy away. She pretended to go to sleep again.

"Tink, if you don't get up, I'll pull the curtains," said Peter. That made Tink move quickly.

Meanwhile the boys were looking sadly at Wendy, Michael and John. They were about to lose their mother.

"Come with us," said Wendy. "I'm sure Mother and Father would adopt you all."

"Really!" they cried, although the invitation had really been aimed at Peter. "Can we go, Peter?"

"All right," said Peter, bitterly. The boys rushed off to pack. Wendy was determined to give Peter some medicine before she left. It was only water but she counted the drops into a cup. She was about to give it to Peter when she saw such a sad look on his face.

"Oh, Peter!" she cried. "Please come with us."

"No," said Peter. "They might make me grow up. I want to stay a boy forever."

"We might find your mother," said Wendy, softly.

Peter no longer missed his mother and told Wendy so. His mind was made up. He would not come with them. The boys were ready.

"Remember to keep your clothes clean," said Wendy. "And don't forget to take your medicine."

"Are you ready, Tink?" asked Peter.

Tink was ready.

"Off you go then," said Peter.

Tink shot up the nearest tree, but no one had time to follow, because the sound of battle suddenly broke out above ground. The pirates had attacked the redskins.

The children all turned to Peter as they heard the sound of clashing steel. The looks on their faces asked Peter not to desert them.

Peter seized his sword. He was ready for battle.

The Children are Captured

The redskins had been taken by surprise. Hook had gone against all the rules of fighting on the island and had attacked at night.

Many of the redskins went to the happy hunting ground that night, but they took some of the pirates with them. The Panther finally managed to break free and clear a path for Tiger Lily and the survivors to escape.

But Hook was not finished. He wanted Pan and Wendy, but mainly Pan. He hated Pan's cockiness. It got on his nerves.

Down below the ground the children waited to hear the outcome of the battle.

"We'll soon know," said Peter. "The redskins will beat a tom-tom to celebrate a win in battle."

Unfortunately, Hook was listening at one of the hollow trees and heard Peter's words. He gave orders for the tom-tom drums to be beaten.

The children cheered and prepared to leave. Hook placed a pirate in front of each hollow tree and there they waited.

The children said goodbye to Peter and climbed into their trees.

The first boy to appear was Curly. As he reached the top of his tree, he arrived in the hands of Cecco. He was thrown to Smee and then onto Starkey, then to Bill Jukes who threw him to Noodler. He landed at Hook's feet. All the other boys were treated in this way.

Wendy was treated differently. She was handed to Hook who raised his hat to her. Then she had to stand by while the boys were being tied up.

The pirates could not tie Slightly up properly. He kept bulging in different places. Hook watched and realised the problem.

Slightly liked to drink water and he had drunk so much his stomach was swollen. Rather than change his shape, Slightly had secretly carved room into

his hollow tree. It was now big enough to take a grown man – a man like Hook.

The boys were thrown in to Wendy's house and the whole house was lifted by the pirates and carried away.

Hook then tiptoed to Slightly's tree and listened. There wasn't a sound. Was Peter Pan asleep or was he waiting at the bottom with a sword drawn ready to kill him? Hook took off his cloak and slipped down the tree.

At the bottom, he looked around the room. Peter was fast asleep on the great bed. He had no idea what had happened above ground. He had played his pipes for a while and had then gone to bed. He had seen the medicine and had ignored it.

He was now fast asleep, a smile on his lips. Hook looked at him and thought what a pretty scene it made. Then he saw the smile. "Odds bods," he thought. "Pan is still cocky even when he is asleep! I can't bear cockiness!"

Hook moved to get into the room, but found that the door to Slightly's tree was shut. The handle was too far down for him to reach.

Then Hook saw Peter's medicine. That was within reach. Hook had an idea. He always carried a small bottle of poison with him. He poured five drops into Peter's medicine.

Then he slipped back up the tree. He wrapped his cloak around him and disappeared into the trees, muttering to himself.

Peter slept on, unaware of what had happened.

At ten o'clock there was a gentle tapping on his tree.

"Who's there," he called, awake at once.

As there was no answer, Peter went to the door.

"I won't open the door, unless you say who you are," he said.

A tinkle of bells answered him. It was Tink.

"What's happened?" asked Peter.

Tink told him what had happened to Wendy and the boys.

"I'll rescue Wendy," cried Peter. But before he set out, he decided to do something that he knew

44

Hook then tiptoed to Slightly's tree and listened.

would please Wendy. He reached for his medicine.

"No!" screamed Tinker bell. She had heard Hook muttering as he had left the underground home. She knew what he'd done. "Hook has poisoned it!"

"Don't be silly," said Peter. "How could he possibly do that?"

"I don't know," cried Tink. "But he has, he has."

Peter would not listen and raised the cup to drink it. Tink flew quickly up and drained the glass herself.

"You've taken my medicine," said Peter, indignantly.

But Tink was already feeling ill. She could hardly fly.

"What's wrong?" asked Peter.

"It was poisoned," whispered Tink. "Now I'm going to die."

"Oh, Tink," said Peter. "You did it to save me, why?"

"You silly boy," she sighed as she flew up to Peter and pinched him on the chin. She then flew to her bed.

Her light was fading. Peter knew if it went out, Tink would be no more. Huge tears rolled down his face.

"What can I do Tink?" asked Peter.

"I think I can get better if the children of the world say they believe in fairies," sighed Tinker Bell.

Peter shouted out to all the children. "Do you believe in fairies?"

They was a reply but it was quite faint.

"Clap if you believe in fairies," called Peter.

That time there was definitely the sound of clapping heard above the house. It worked. Tink was saved, her light grew brighter and in no time she jumped up.

"Now to rescue Wendy," said Peter.

Outside it had been snowing. Peter crept through the woods, travelling like the redskins. He did not want anyone to see him.

He dashed through the moonlight, dagger ready. Peter Pan was as happy as he could be.

46

The Pirate Ship

The moon shone over the Jolly Roger, as it lay moored in Kidd's Creek.

Hook was on the main deck, deep in thought. Pan was dead and the boys were about to walk the plank.

Hook yelled to his men. "Are the boys chained? I don't want any of them flying away."

"Aye, aye, Captain," said the pirates.

"Bring them on deck," Hook bellowed.

The boys were dragged from the hold and stood in front of Hook. Wendy told them to be brave, but they were just small boys.

"Now then," said Hook. "Six of you must walk the plank tonight, but I need two young cabin boys."

"Well sir," said Tootles, stepping forward. "I don't think my mother would like me to be a pirate. Would your mother, Slightly?"

"No," said Slightly. None of the other boys thought so, either.

"Then it's the plank for you all," said Hook. Turning to his men, he ordered, "Get the plank ready and bring up their mother."

47

"Is this mutiny?" asked Hook. "Come, shake hands with me, Starkey."

Starkey knew what would happen. He made a run for it and dived over the side of the ship.

"Four," said Slightly.

Hook grabbed a light and went into the cabin.

Slightly would have loved to say "five," but Hook came out again, looking slightly puzzled.

"Something blew my light out," he said.

The pirates were not keen to go in the cabin and talk of mutiny began.

The pirates began to panic and the children cheered.

Hook looked at them. "Lads," he cried to his crew. "Let's send the children in. If they kill this crowing thing, we're saved. If it kills them, it's saved us a job."

The boys were pushed, pretending to struggle, into the cabin and the door was closed.

"Listen," said Hook. The pirates listened, but with their backs turned. Meanwhile, Peter freed the boys from their chains, armed them and then let them out of the cabin with orders to hide themselves.

Peter flew to the mast and freed Wendy. Then he put on her cloak and took her place. Wendy hid with the boys. Peter took a deep breath and crowed.

The pirates were panic stricken. Had the creature killed all the boys?

"There's a Jonah on board, lads," said Hook.

"It's the girl. A girl always brings bad luck to a pirate ship. Throw her overboard."

The pirates rushed at the mast and Mullins cried out, "No one can save you now!"

"One person can," said a voice from beneath the cloak.

"Who's that?" asked Mullins, puzzled.

"Peter Pan, the avenger!" cried Peter Pan, flinging off the cloak. The pirates were amazed. Hook was speechless, then he found his voice. "Kill him, lads!" he cried.

"Down boys and at them!" cried Peter. The boys

50

flew in from all corners of the ship. The pirates were so surprised they struck out at anything. Some tried to hide, others leapt into the sea.

Slightly ran around with a lantern showing the hidden pirates. They were quickly picked off. Slightly was busy counting with each splash and screech. "-five-six-seven-eight-nine-ten-eleven-"

Finally only Hook was left and he was surrounded by the boys. They closed in on him but kept out of reach of the wicked hook.

"This one's mine," said Peter, as he joined the circle of boys.

The boys stepped back and the two lifelong enemies gazed at each other.

"Prepare to meet your doom," said Hook.

The fight began. Peter was a superb swordsman, but he was much smaller than Hook, so he could never quite reach his target.

Hook was surprised at how good Peter was and began to use his hook as well. It flashed through the air nearly slicing Peter in two and Hook came in closer for the kill.

Peter let Hook come closer, then darted in with his sword. He wounded Hook on the ribs.

If there was one thing Hook hated, it was the sight of his own blood and he dropped his sword in panic.

"Now!" cried the boys.

But Peter was fair and let Hook pick up his sword and the fight continued.

Hook was desperate, wondering what he was fighting against. He was wounded in the ribs again. It was too much for him. He rushed to a barrel of gunpowder, lit a fuse and dropped it in.

"There!" he cried "The ship will be blown to bits!"

But Peter flew over and threw the fuse into the water.

The boys flew up into the rigging and began to torment Hook from the air, stabbing at him. The Captain staggered about, blindly lashing out at the boys who always stayed just out of reach. Peter closed in on Hook again. The pirate captain

51

The Captain staggered about, blindly lashing out at the boys
who always stayed just out of reach.

"Oh, Nana," she cried, as she woke up. "I dreamed the children had returned." Tears were in Nana's eyes as well.

Mr Darling returned, kennel and all and was back in the nursery.

"It has been a long day, my dear," said Mr Darling. "Would you play the piano for me?"

Mrs Darling went to the nursery piano.

"There is a draught. Can you close the window?" asked Mr Darling.

Mrs Darling was horrified. "Never ask me to do that," she said. "It must always be left open for them."

She began to play and Mr Darling fell asleep.

As he slept Peter Pan and Tinker Bell flew into the room. But where were the children? Surely they should have arrived as well.

"Quick Tink, close and bar the window," said Peter.

Peter and Tink hid. When Wendy arrived she would think her mother had forgotten her. Then she would have to go back to Neverland with Peter. This was the way Peter Pan planned it.

Peter looked at Mrs Darling playing the piano "You'll never see Wendy again, he whispered. He saw two big tears appear in her eyes as she finished playing the song.

'She wants me to open the window,' thought Peter. 'Well, I won't.'

The next time Peter looked, the tears were running down Mrs Darling's cheeks. 'She's very fond of Wendy,' thought Peter. 'Well, so am I.'

"Oh, all right," he finally said. "If she wants Wendy, we'll have to let her in."

They both flew up and opened the window. Moments later, Wendy, Michael and John flew in.

"I think I've been here before," said Michael.

"Of course you have," said John. "There's your bed."

"Oh, yes," said Michael.

"Look," said John. "There's the kennel." He went to look inside. "Oh, there's a man in there."

"It's Father!" cried Wendy. "What is he doing in there?"

"He never used to sleep in there, did he?" said John.

"Maybe we just don't remember clearly," said Wendy.

Mrs Darling finished playing and walked towards the beds. All were now occupied.

Mrs Darling had seen them, but could not believe her eyes. She had dreamed of their return so often, she thought this was another dream.

She sat in the chair by the fire.

"Mother!" called Wendy.

"That's Wendy's voice," said Mrs Darling.

"Mother!" called John and Michael.

"Those are John's and Michael's voices," said Mrs Darling, and she dreamily held out her arms.

Wendy, John and Michael slipped from their beds and stood before her. Her arms went around them and she realised that she was holding her children again.

Mr Darling woke up to see the children again. Nana came in. There could not have been a happier scene and there was no one to see it, except for a strange little boy at the window.

Poor Peter Pan. This was one joy and adventure that he would never know.

Meanwhile the lost boys had also arrived. They were standing at the front door, waiting until Wendy had had a chance to tell her mother about them. Then they went in. They were soon standing

There could not have been a happier scene . . .

in front of Mrs Darling.

Mrs Darling could see how much they wanted to stay.

"They must stay," she told Mr Darling.

"You don't do things by halves, do you Wendy?" said Mr Darling.

The twins thought he must mean them. "We can go away, if you think we will be too much trouble," said one of the twins.

"Father!" cried Wendy.

"We could sleep doubled up," said Nibs.

Mr Darling was glad to welcome them, but would have liked to have been asked first.

"We'll find room for you in the drawing room," he announced.

"We'll squeeze in," said the boys.

"Off we go, then," and Mr Darling led the way into the house and they all fitted in somewhere.

Wendy spoke to Peter once more that evening. He came to say goodbye.

Wendy was sad. "Are you really going?" she asked.

"Yes," said Peter.

Mrs Darling came up to the window.

"I'm adopting the boys," she said. "We can adopt you, too."

"Would you send me to school?" asked Peter.

"Yes," said Mrs Darling.

"And then to work?"

59

"I suppose so."

"So, I would grow up to be a man?" asked Peter.

"Yes, of course," said Mrs Darling.

"Ugh!" said Peter. "I don't want to grow up. I never want to be a man or grow a beard!"

"But where will you live?" asked Wendy.

"In the house we built, on the island," said Peter. "The fairies will put it in the treetops for us."

"Won't you be lonely?" asked Wendy.

"You could come back with me, if you think that," said Peter.

Wendy looked at her mother.

"I've only just got you back," said her mother. "I don't want to lose you again."

"He does need a mother," said Wendy.

"So do you, my love," said Mrs Darling.

"Oh, all right," said Peter. But Mrs Darling could see that he would miss Wendy.

"Why don't you come back in the spring and Wendy can help you with the spring-cleaning?" suggested Mrs Darling.

Peter was delighted, but he had no sense of time, so he may return or he may not. Now he was going.

"You won't forget me, will you, Peter?" said Wendy. "Promise you won't forget spring-cleaning time."

"I promise," called Peter as he flew off with Tink flying beside him.

The boys went to school and soon settled to an ordinary life. They soon lost the skill of flying. Nana had to tie their feet to the bedpost at first. But soon they forgot or they did not believe.

Spring came and Peter came for Wendy. She was worried because she had grown so much, but Peter did not notice.

The following year Peter did not come.

"Maybe there's no such person as Peter Pan," suggested Michael. Wendy could not believe this.

She was delighted when the following year Peter came back. He did not know he had missed a year. But that was the last time Wendy saw Peter as a

young girl.

The years passed and the children grew up. Tootles became a judge, Michael became an engine driver and Slightly married and became a lord.

Wendy married and had a daughter, Jane.

One night, Jane had a strange visitor. It was Peter Pan.

Wendy had told her daughter all the stories about Peter Pan, so Jane knew immediately who it was. She was not scared.

"I've come to collect my mother," he told Jane.

"I know," said Jane. "I've been waiting."

Wendy came into the nursery to see Peter and Jane talking.

"She is my mother," said Peter.

"He does need a mother," said Jane, flying round the room.

"I know," said Wendy.

"Goodbye," said Peter and he flew up to join Jane.

"It's only for spring-cleaning," said Jane.

"If only I could come too," said Wendy.

"But you can't fly," said Jane.

Wendy let them go and watched from the nursery window as they flew off into the sky.

Many years have passed since then. Wendy is now old and has grey hair and Jane has a daughter of her own, Margaret.

Margaret flies to Neverland with Peter and tells him stories about himself and the fairies, Captain Hook and the redskins. He cannot remember the adventures, but he loves to hear the stories.

When Margaret grows up, she will probably have a daughter who will be Peter Pan's mother. It will probably go on this way, for as long as children believe in fairies.